the horse rider . . .

the barber

. . . and the horse

the groom

the little ghost

the bride

the girl who likes
to swing in trees

the writer

The Ghost Catcher

~ *A Bengali Folktale* ~

Martha Hamilton & Mitch Weiss • Illustrated by Kristen Balouch

AUGUST HOUSE
Little folk
ATLANTA

Published 2008 by August House LittleFolk
3500 Piedmont Road NE, Suite 310, Atlanta, Georgia 30305
404-442-4420
http://www.augusthouse.com

Book Design by Shock Design & Associates, Inc.

Manufactured in Korea

10 9 8 7 6 5 4 3 2 1

LIBRARY OF CONGRESS CATALOGING-IN-PUBLICATION DATA

Hamilton, Martha.
 The ghost catcher : a Bengali folktale / Martha Hamilton & Mitch Weiss; illustrated
by Kristen Balouch.
     p. cm.
 Summary: A retelling of a traditional Bengali tale in which a kind and generous
Indian barber, pressed by his wife to earn more money, cleverly persuades a ghost to
bring him riches.
 ISBN 978-0-87483-835-0 (hardcover : alk. paper) [1. Folklore—India.] I. Weiss,
Mitch, 1951–. II. Balouch, Kristen, ill. III. Title.

  PZ8.1.H1535Gho 2008
  398.20954—dc22
  [E]

                        2007014308

The paper used in this publication meets the minimum requirements of the
American National Standard for Information Sciences—Permanence of Paper
for Printed Library Materials, ANSI Z39.48-1984.

Lesson plans available at www.augusthouse.com

AUGUST HOUSE, INC.
ATLANTA

For Mom, who in her 90th year
dazzles us daily with her joie de vivre.

— **MW & MH**

For Omid

— **KB**

In a small village in Bengal

there lived a young barber who loved his work. As he cut hair and trimmed beards, he heard many entertaining stories. But if a customer told him a tale of woe, the barber would say, "Keep your money. You need it more than I do." So on most days, he returned home without a single coin.

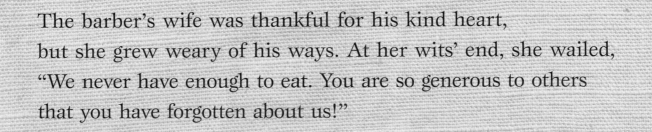

The barber's wife was thankful for his kind heart,
but she grew weary of his ways. At her wits' end, she wailed,
"We never have enough to eat. You are so generous to others
that you have forgotten about us!"

She picked up the bag that held his scissors, combs,
and mirrors and thrust it into his hands.
"Don't come back until you can promise
that we will not go hungry again."

The barber decided to go
to the next village.
It would be easier to accept
money from strangers.
So he took his bag of tools
and set off on the long walk.
As night fell, the barber
passed a large banyan tree.
*This will be a perfect place
to sleep for the night,*
he thought.

It happened that a ghost lived in that tree.
As soon as the barber fell asleep, the ghost
glided down and let out a hideous laugh.
"HA HA HA HA HA!
You will make a tasty meal!"
The barber jolted awake.

In spite of his fright, the barber thought quickly.

"HA HA HA HA HA!" he screeched back.

"I have no fear of you. I am a ghost catcher!"

He pulled a large mirror from his bag

and stuck it in front of the ghost's face.

"Look at this gruesome ghost I have already caught.

You will soon join him in my magical bag.

Don't bother trying to escape.

My bag will find you no matter where you hide."

The ghost had never seen a mirror.
He did not recognize his own reflection!
Filled with fear, he begged,
"Kind sir, **I'll do whatever you say!**
Please don't put me in that bag with that ugly ghost!"

"Fine," replied the barber.
"Tonight I am going to sleep under your tree.
By morning, I want you to bring me one thousand gold *mohor*.
Otherwise, it's into my bag you go!"

The ghost took one look at the bag and flew off in a frenzy.

When the barber awoke, the ghost
presented him with a pot of gold *mohor*.

"Well done!" marveled the barber. "But I have one more command. Build a shed by my house and fill it with rice by tomorrow. Then I will release you from my spell."

"**Tomorrow**?" whined the ghost. "**That's impossible**!"

"It is cither that," warned the barber, "or you will live in my bag forever."

With a gasp, the ghost flew off in a flash.

When the barber returned home, he showed his wife the pot of gold *mohor* and told her of his meeting with the ghost. "Dear, I am impressed by your cleverness," laughed his wife. She was thrilled to know that their worries were over.

The ghost worked from morning till night.

After he finished building the shed, he filled it with bag upon bag of rice.

While he was working, his uncle floated by.

The uncle had never seen a ghost work so hard.

Horrified, he cried, "**What are you doing**?"

"A powerful human being lives in that house," whimpered the nephew. "He is a ghost catcher. I must finish this task by the end of the day. Otherwise, he will put me into a bag with a ghastly ghost he has already captured."

The uncle was ashamed of his nephew.
**"You fool! Human beings have no power over us.
Come with me! I will teach this man to have proper respect for ghosts."**

The two ghosts peered into the window of the barber's house.

The uncle ghost let out his most horrifying cackle:

"HA HA HA HA HA!

What a scrumptious snack this human will be!

Shall we eat him now, nephew?

Or perhaps we should wait and cook him in our curry!"

To the uncle's surprise, the barber showed no fear.

He calmly strolled to the window and looked at the nephew.

"Since you have done all that I demanded, you are free to go."

Then he glared at the uncle.

"But your fiendish friend must take your place in my bag."

The uncle ghost was enraged.

"How dare you talk to a ghost like that!" he shrieked.

But just then, the barber whipped out his largest mirror.

He held it in front of the uncle's face.

"How would you like to spend the rest of your days with this frightful creature?" he warned.

The uncle ghost
was no smarter than his nephew.
"**Oh, sir**," he pleaded, "**whatever you do, don't put me
in the bag with that disgusting ghost! I will bring you two
thousand gold *mohor* and build you a bigger shed filled with rice**."

"If you do that," replied the barber, "I will be satisfied."

The uncle ghost kept his promise. Afterward, he and his nephew
turned and flew the other way whenever they saw the barber coming.

From then on,
the barber spent his days cheerfully cutting hair,
trimming beards, and listening to wonderful stories.
But what truly delighted him was knowing he had more than enough
to share with those in need.

❧ *About the Story* ❧

Throughout India, barbers (*napeet*) traditionally traveled about
to cut the hair of regular customers. To this day, a barber
"shop" is often nothing more than a pair of scissors, a mirror, and
a chair (or perhaps just a stack of bricks or stone) on the street, in
a busy market, or in the shade of a banyan tree. Here men gather
to gossip, read the newspaper, and tell stories.

When bedtime draws near in Bengal, grandmothers (*thaakuma*)
gather the young ones and tell age-old stories. These are tales of lofty
kings (*raja*) and powerful goddesses (*debi*); of common folks such as
farmers (*chaashi*) and barbers; and of the supernatural including
ghosts (*bhoot*) of many kinds. The nephew and uncle "ghosts" in
this tale are most likely demons called *rakshasa* (literally "destroyer").
This particular kind of demon rules the forest and feeds on human
flesh. *Rakshasa* are shape shifters who take a variety of forms.
They may have extra limbs or missing limbs, and even though
they are menacing, they are not terribly bright.

This story was retold from "The Ghost Who Was Afraid of
Being Bagged" from *Folk-Tales of Bengal* by Rev. Lal Behari Day
(London: Macmillan, 1889) and "The Barber and the
Ghost" from *Indian Folklore* by Ram Satya Mukharji
(Calcutta: Sanyal, 1904).

the poet's grandbaby

the school boy

the poet

the barber's papa

the baker

the uncle ghost

the barber's wife